For Marion Clapham
JW

Little Hare Books
4/21 Mary Street, Surry Hills
NSW 2010 AUSTRALIA

Copyright © John Winch 2005

First published in 2005

National Library of Australia
Cataloguing-in-Publication entry

Winch, John, 1944-.
Run, hare, run! : the story of a drawing.

For children.
ISBN 1 877003 87 5.

1. Dürer, Albrecht, 1471-1528 - Juvenile fiction.
2. Artists - Germany - Juvenile fiction. 3. Hares in art -
Juvenile fiction. I. Title.

A823.3

Design by Serious Business
Produced by Phoenix Offset, Hong Kong
Printed in China

5 4 3 2 1

Run, Hare, Run!
The story of a drawing

John Winch

LITTLE HARE

A long time ago, by the edge of a forest, lived a wild brown hare.

One day, a hunter and his hound came from the nearby city.
The hare crouched low, hiding in the long grass by the roots
of an old oak tree, but the hound picked up his scent.
Run, hare, run!

The hare ran out of the forest and across the fields.

When he searched for shelter in the farmyard,

the animals raised a ruckus and gave him away.

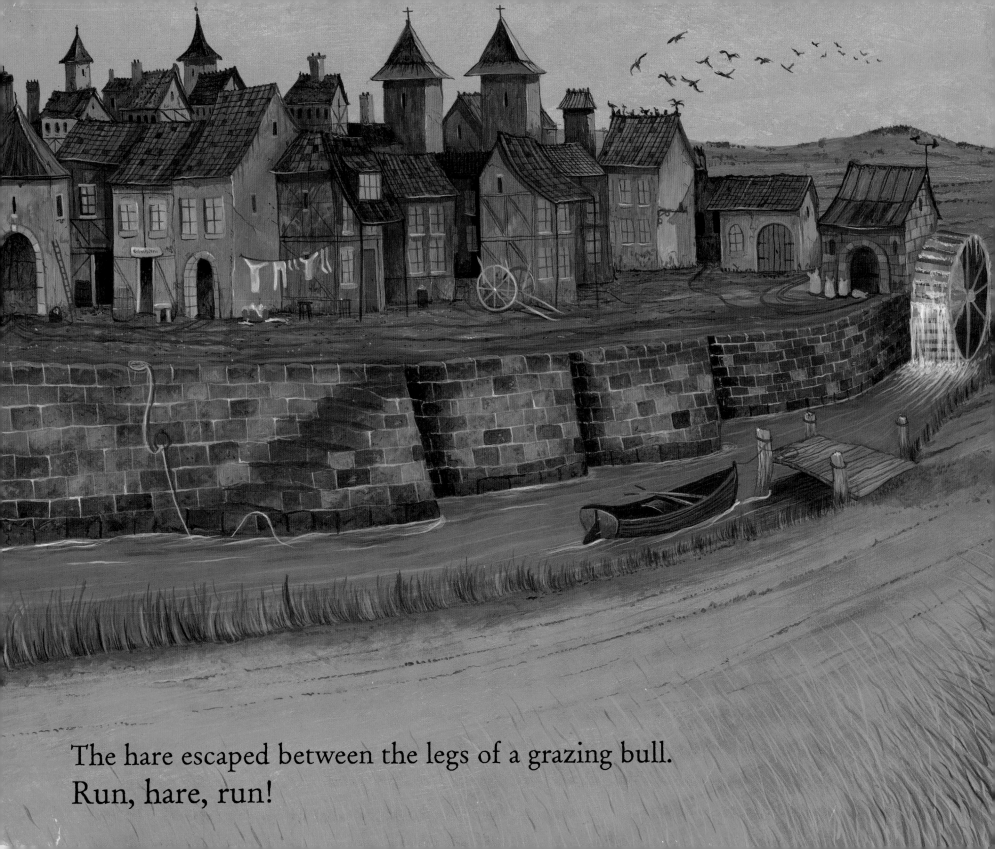

The hare escaped between the legs of a grazing bull.
Run, hare, run!

He dived into the moat that surrounded
the city and swam its icy waters.

He tried to lose the hound in the cobbled
maze of streets and lanes.

The hare sought
sanctuary in the
darkened cathedral.
Run, hare, run!

He hid in the midst of the crowd in the busy market square.

Exhausted, the hare lay down in a barn,
and that's where he was discovered...

and caught.

The hunter lowered the hare into a basket
and carried him home. The hare trembled with fear
and shivered with cold as the hunter prepared his tools.

But the gentle voice of the hunter soothed him
and he sat as still as stone all through the night…

until the dawn light led him home.

The hunter became a great artist and lived a long and happy life.
And the wild brown hare lives forever.

1502

DÜRER
—
1471 - 1528

Author's note

Thousands of paintings line the walls of galleries and museums throughout the world. Some portray great battles and heroic deeds, while others depict simple scenes of gentle rolling hills and tranquil villages. Proud kings and queens in regal costumes and peasants eating a midday meal hang side by side for eternity. The only thing these paintings have in common is that each represents an instant of time caught forever by the artist. But hidden in the brushstrokes of each painting is another story—the story of the artist and his subject.

Since I first set eyes on a reproduction of *The Hare* by Albrecht Dürer I have been attracted by its simplicity and grace, and wondered about the story behind the drawing…Little is known about the picture—was it drawn from life, or from a museum specimen?—but the artist's love of nature is evident in his simple and economical rendering of the hare. Personally, I am sure it was drawn from life!

The original drawing is in the Albertina Museum in Vienna and, due to its fragility, is only exhibited very rarely. I was lucky enough to see *The Hare* in 2003. This book is my attempt, as an author and illustrator, to understand it.

Albrecht Dürer was born in Nuremberg, Germany in 1471, the son of a goldsmith. By the time he died in 1528, he was one of Nuremberg's richest men and most respected artists.